GET BUSY, BEAVER!

BY **CAROLYN CRIMI**

ILLUSTRATED BY **JANIE BYNUM**

Orchard Books • New York
An Imprint of Scholastic Inc.

Library of Congress Cataloging-in-Publication Data
Crimi, Carolyn; Bynum, Janie, ill. Get busy, Beaver! / by Carolyn Crimi
illustrated by Janie Bynum. p.   cm. 0-439-54866-7
2003020120

1 2 3 4 5 6 7 8 9 10   04 05 06 07 08

Printed in Singapore   46 • First edition, October 2004
Book design by David Caplan and Yvette Awad
The display type was set in Goudy Stout. The text type was set in 18-point Elroy.

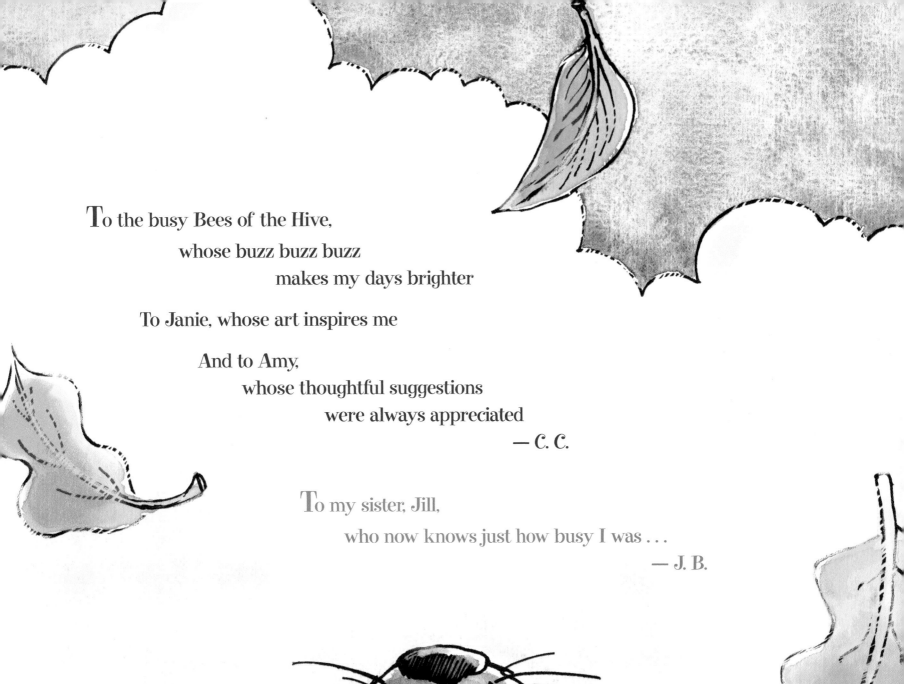

To the busy Bees of the Hive,
whose buzz buzz buzz
makes my days brighter

To Janie, whose art inspires me

And to Amy,
whose thoughtful suggestions
were always appreciated
— C. C.

To my sister, Jill,
who now knows just how busy I was . . .
— J. B.

It was fall, and the Beaver family was busy, busy, busy rebuilding their dam.

"Go, go, go," said Pa Beaver.

"Now, now, now," said Ma Beaver.

"Fast, fast, fast," said Sister Babs Beaver.

Thelonious Beaver started to help out, but he stopped to watch a cloud that looked like a flower, and another one that looked like a leaf, and another, and another, and another, until suddenly the afternoon was over.

"Oh, Thelonious," said Pa Beaver.
"You need to stop daydreaming!"

On the other side of the
pond, a new family of
beavers started rebuilding
their dam.

Pa Beaver worried.
"Build, build, build,"
he told his family.

Ma Beaver agreed.

"Quick, quick, quick," she said.

"Chop, chop, chop," said Babs Beaver.

Thelonious tried to help out, but he stopped to watch
the way the leaves swirled and twirled in circles
on the water and how the dragonflies
skimmed across it, and pretty
soon the afternoon was over.

"Oh, Thelonious," said Ma Beaver.
"You need to get busy!"

On the other side of the pond, the new family of beavers worked harder on their dam.

Pa Beaver worried. "It's bigger," he said.

"It's wider," said Ma Beaver.

"It's better," said Babs Beaver.

With a flip-flapping of tails
and a chomp-chomping
of teeth,

Pa, Ma, and Babs
Beaver got busy,
busy, busy.

Every day, their dam
grew bigger and wider
and better.

Every night, they slept hard, tired from their work. . .
Except Thelonious, who watched the stars blink and
the fireflies wink until he drifted off to sleep.

"Thelonious, wake up!
Time to get to work!" said Babs.

Thelonious waddled toward the water in his sleepy, dreamy way. He never moved very fast. He didn't want to miss one single flower or leaf.

Flap, flap, flap

went the tails of the Beaver family.

Chomp, chomp, chomp

went the teeth of the Beaver family.

Their dam grew bigger and wider. But no matter what Pa, Ma, and Babs Beaver did, the dam across the way seemed better.

"Build, build, build!"
"Chop, chop, chop!"
"Fast, fast, fast!"

"THELONIOUS! GET BUSY!"

Thelonious wanted to help out, but other things kept getting in his way. Like the feel of rough bark, or the buzz of a bumblebee, or the shape of a spider's web.

He watched and listened and smelled until an idea came to him in a very slow,
Thelonious kind of way. The idea grew and grew until Thelonious had no choice
but to start working on it.

The rest of the Beaver family worked
harder and harder on their dam. They
were so busy, busy, busy with their
building, building, building
that they didn't notice Thelonious
was hardly ever there.

Then one day, they found something new in the pond.

Pa swam toward it.

Ma swam around it.

Babs climbed one of its branches.

They did not say a word.

They gazed at it and sniffed at it and explored it with their teeth and paws.

"What is it?" asked Pa Beaver.

"Where did it come from?" asked Ma Beaver.

"How did it get here?" asked Babs Beaver.

The beavers from across the
way were curious, too. Soon
both families were exploring it
from all sides. They climbed on
its branches. They smelled the
tart leaves and listened to
the flutter and hum of
its butterflies and bees.

"It's a forest," said one beaver.

"It's a garden," said another.

"It's a masterpiece," said a third.

"I bet Thelonious will know exactly what it is," said Babs Beaver.

Just then, Thelonious swam up and added some brightly colored leaves.

"Oh, Thelonious,"
Ma Beaver said. "You *have* been busy!"

No one built that day. No tails flapped. No teeth chomped. The pond was quiet and still as all the beavers admired Thelonious's creation.

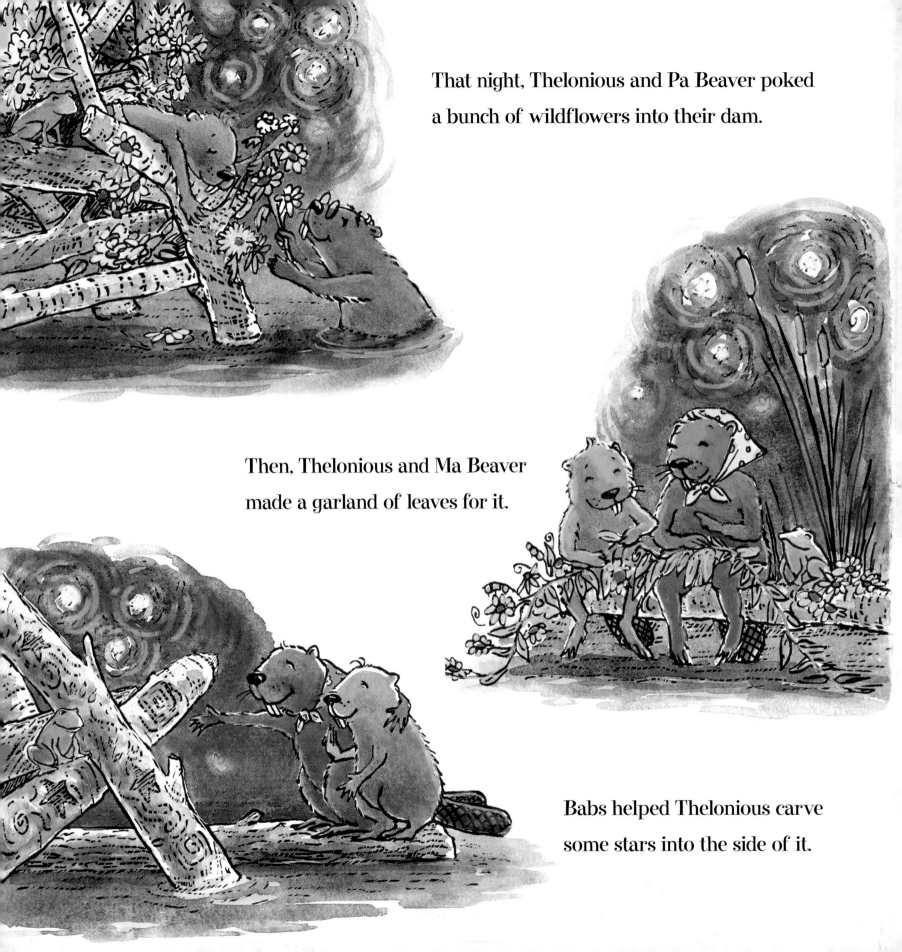

That night, Thelonious and Pa Beaver poked a bunch of wildflowers into their dam.

Then, Thelonious and Ma Beaver made a garland of leaves for it.

Babs helped Thelonious carve some stars into the side of it.

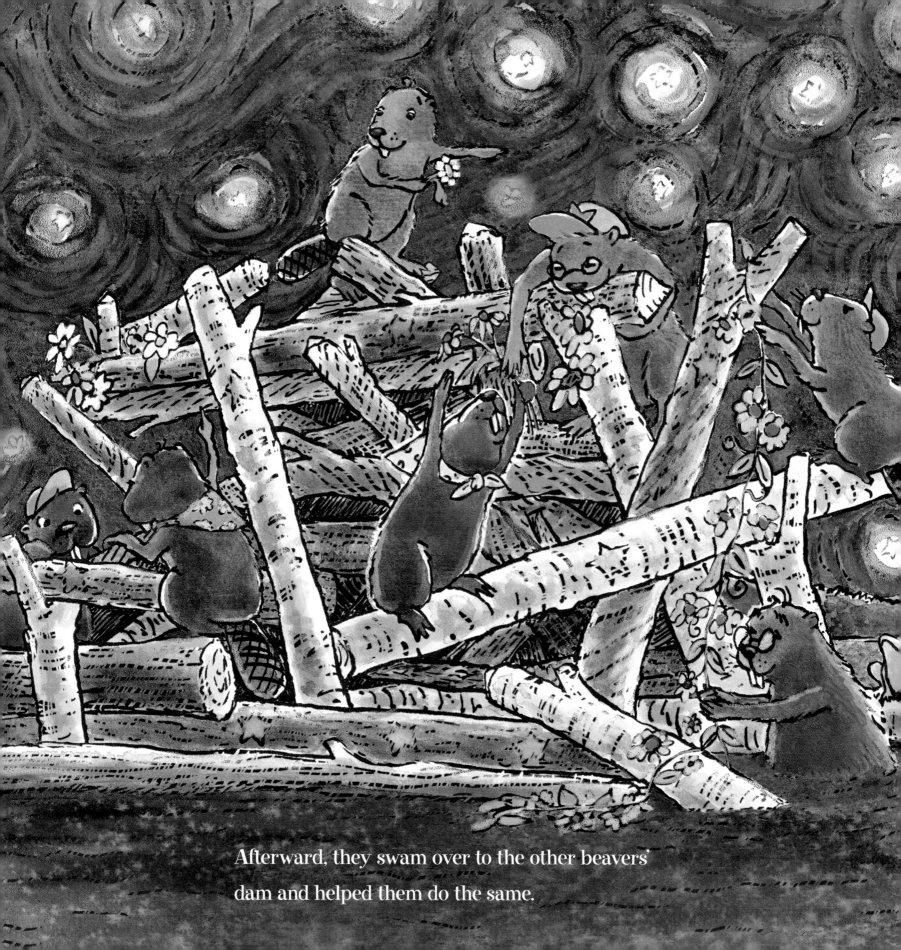

Afterward, they swam over to the other beavers'
dam and helped them do the same.

The Beavers slept a peaceful night of dreams. . . .

All except Thelonious, who quietly and slowly went to work again.